Based on the book "The Hundred and One Dalmatians" by Dodie Smith,
published by The Viking Press

A GOLDEN BOOK®
Western Publishing Company, Inc.
Racine, Wisconsin 53404

PONGO & ROGER

PERDITA & ANITA

ROGER & ANITA

PONGO & PERDITA

PATCH

PUPPY
BISCUITS
ROLLY

LUCKY

PENNY

SPOT

Draw your favorite pup!

HORACE
JASPER

CRUELLA

Which dog goes with which owner?
Can you find the ones that match?

Answers: A-2, B-1, C-3, D-4

1
2
3
4

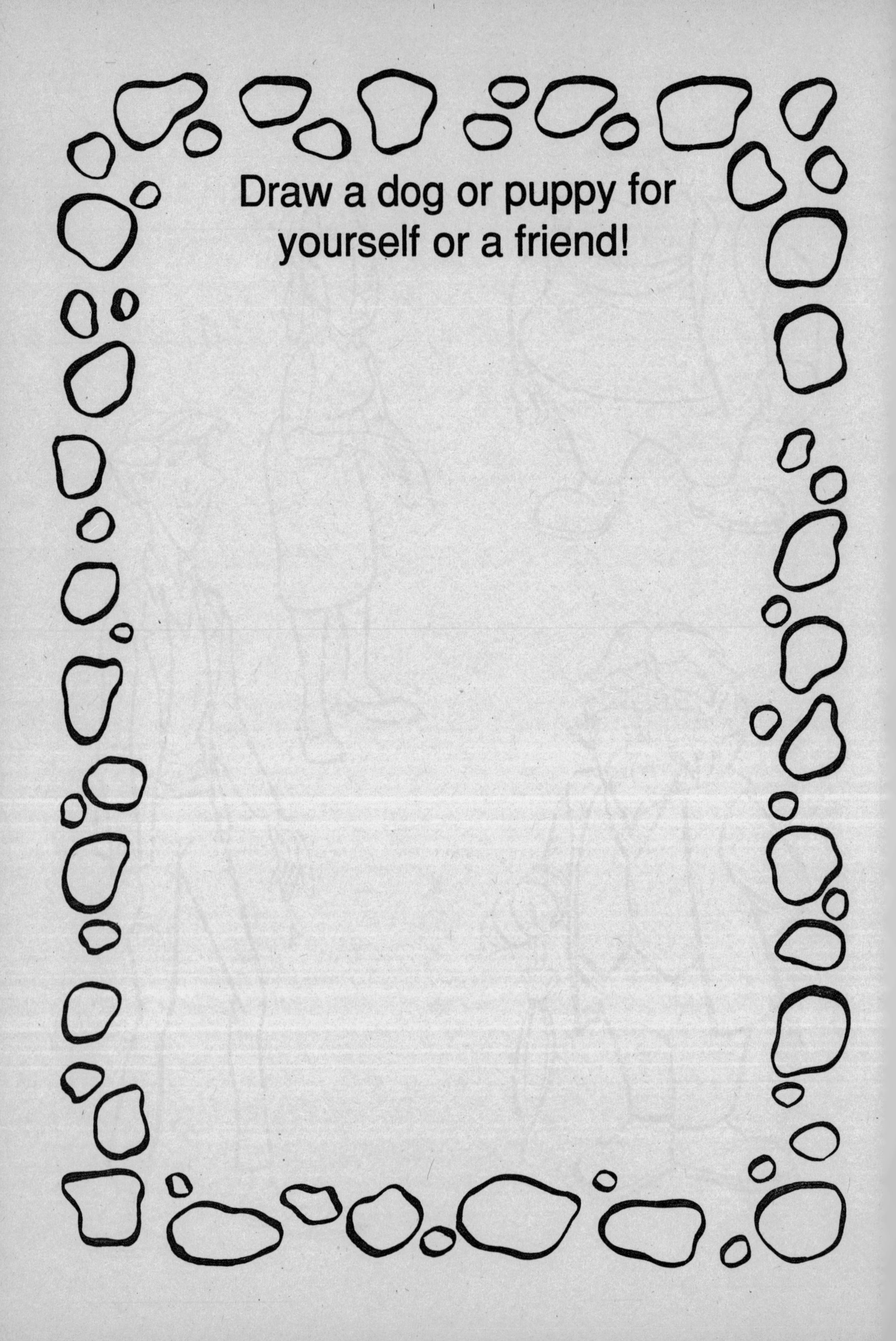
Draw a dog or puppy for
yourself or a friend!

Help Pongo lead Roger to Anita and Perdy.

What do Pongo and Perdy dream about? A juicy bone? Their 15 puppies? Draw what you think is on their minds.

Who's at the door? Connect the dots.

Dalmatian puppies aren't born with spots.
Can you give the new puppies their spots?

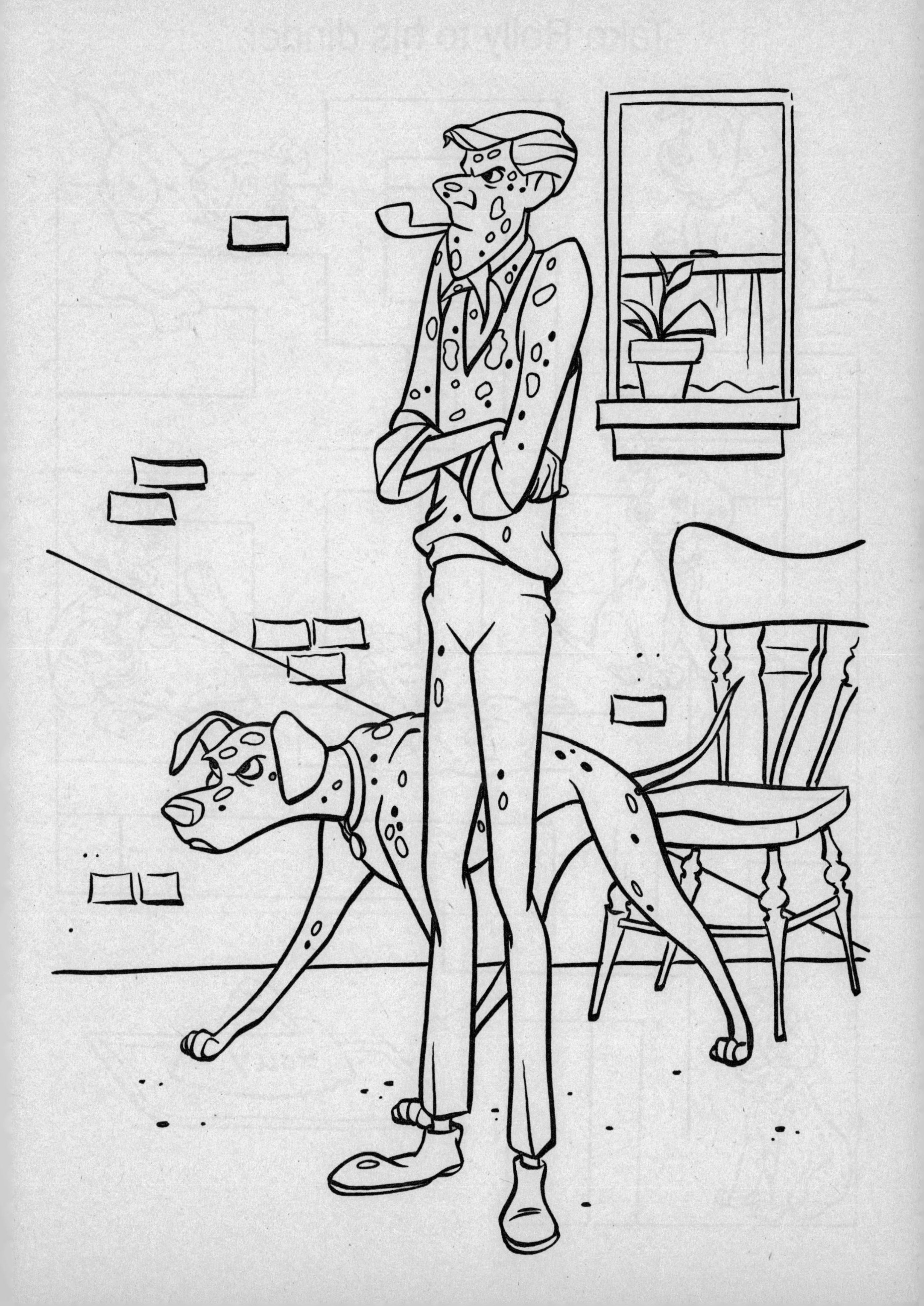

Take Rolly to his dinner.

Which 2 puppies are exactly the same?

Answer: Number 1 and number 5

Find all 15 puppies.
Some of them are hiding!

Help Perdy take Lucky to bed.

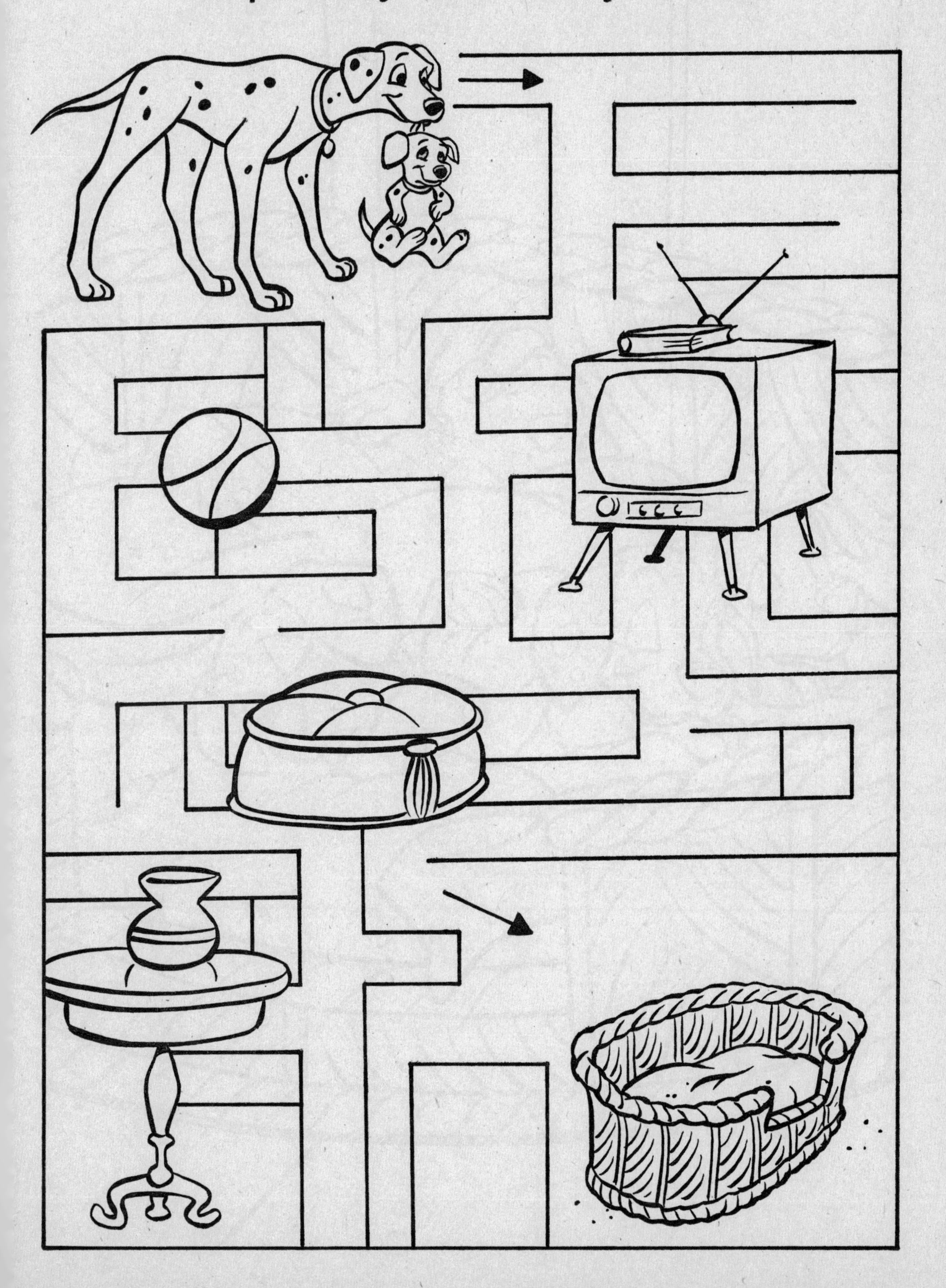

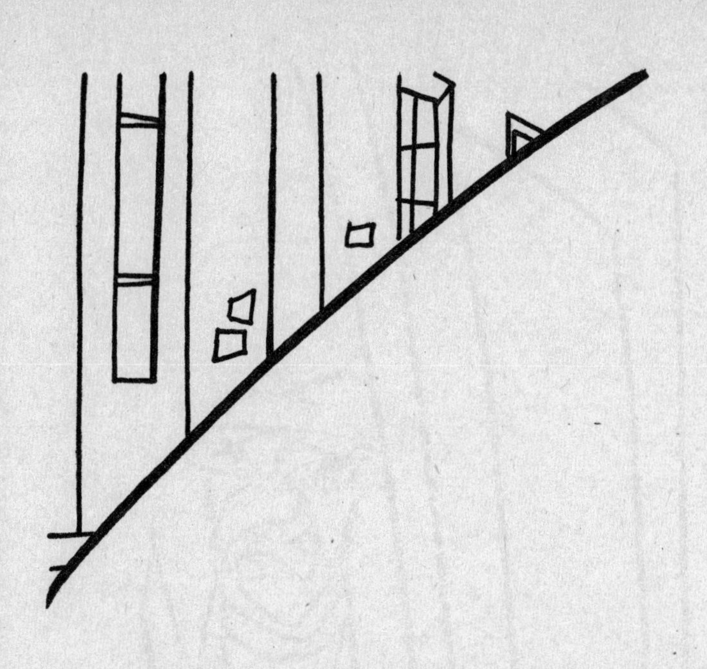

Connect the dots.

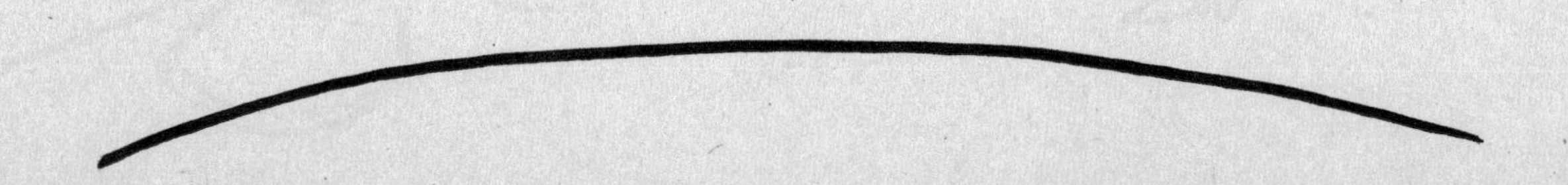

Get Nanny to the pups' basket
to discover the crime!

What's wrong
with this picture?
STOP
CAFE

Connect the dots.

Take Sergeant Tibs
to investigate the mansion.

What is Jasper drinking?
Connect the dots.

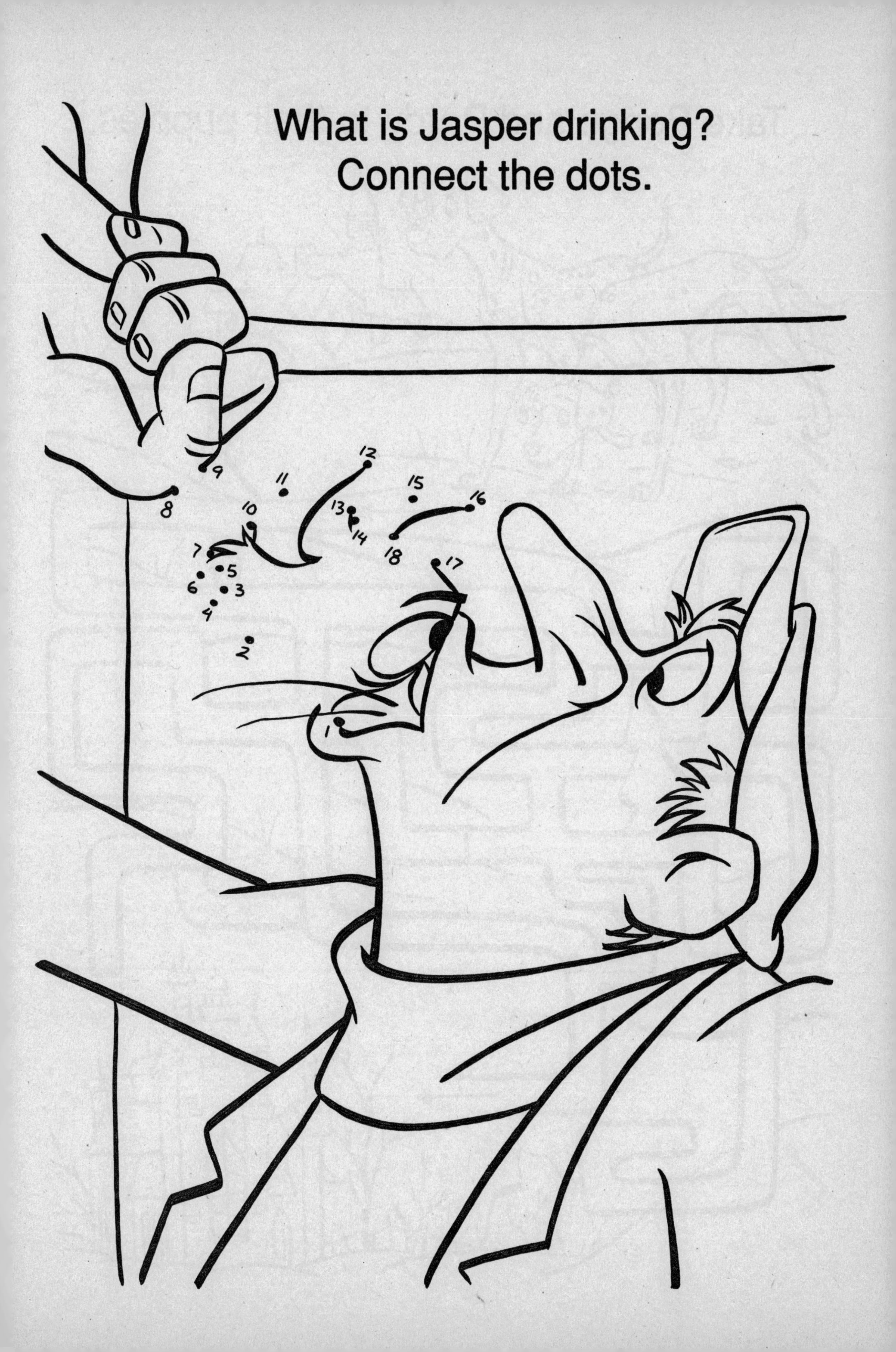

Take Pongo and Perdy to their puppies.

What's wrong with this picture?

Help Lucky get to
his favorite TV show.

Which way did the puppies go?
Follow their footprints to find out.

Help disguise the puppies --
color them black.